PRIME Baby

PRIME Baby

GENE LUEN YANG

COLORS BY
DEREK KIRK KIM

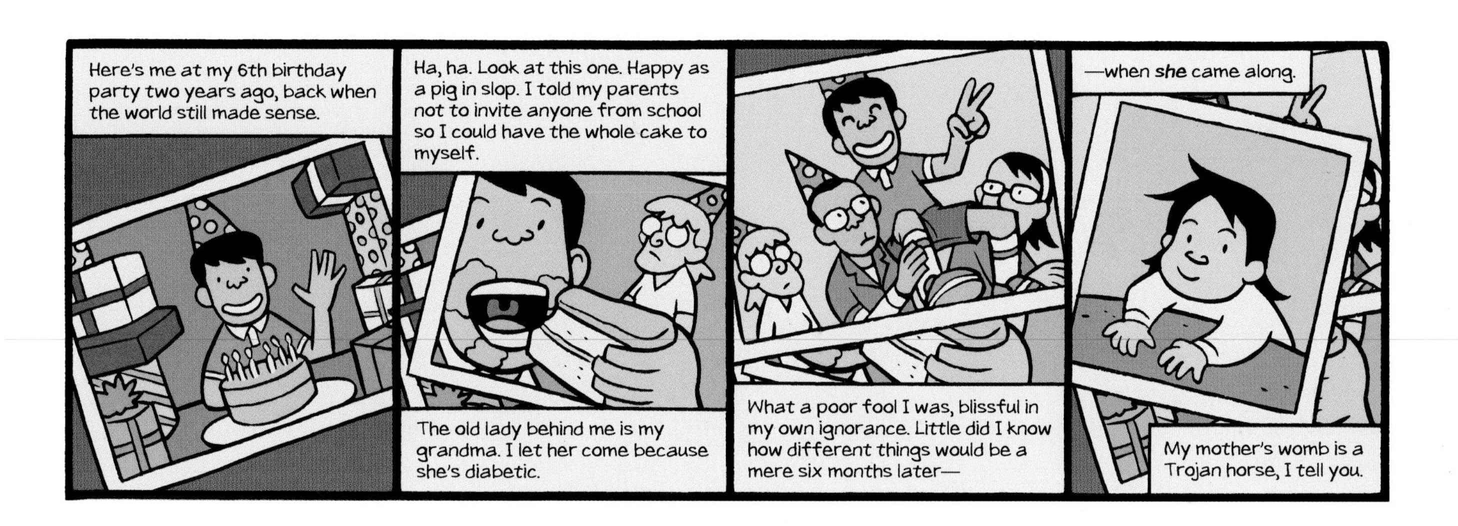
Here's me at my 6th birthday party two years ago, back when the world still made sense.
Ha, ha. Look at this one. Happy as a pig in slop. I told my parents not to invite anyone from school so I could have the whole cake to myself.
The old lady behind me is my grandma. I let her come because she's diabetic.
What a poor fool I was, blissful in my own ignorance. Little did I know how different things would be a mere six months later—
—when *she* came along.
My mother's womb is a Trojan horse, I tell you.

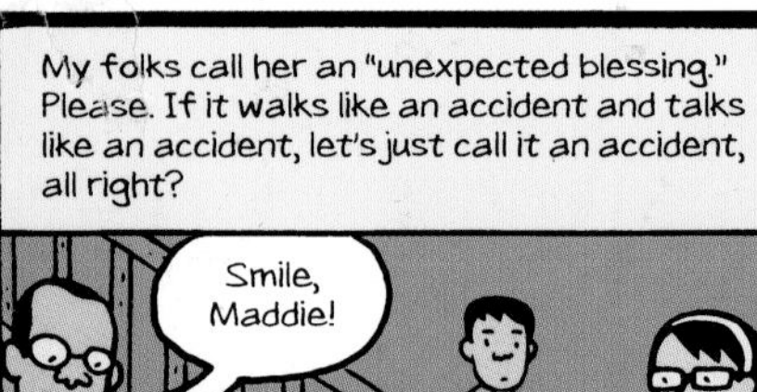

I know what you're thinking. You think I'm just jealous of all the attention those fat little baby cheeks of hers are getting. But that's not it. That's not it at all.

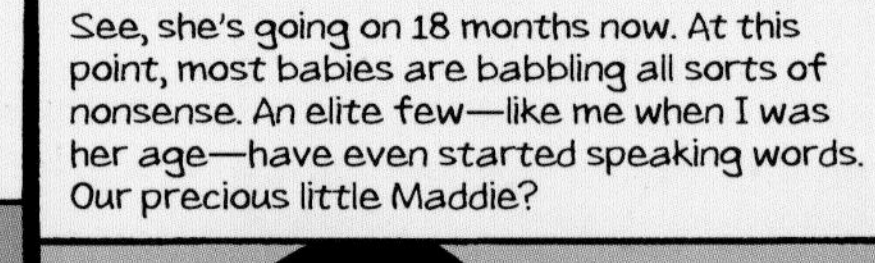

That's it. Seriously. No "ooh." No "ah." No "mama" or "papa." Just "ga," over and over and over again.

All day.
Ga ga.
All night.
Ga ga ga ga ga ga ga ga ga ga ga ga ga.
Is that a sign of something mental or what?
When I mention this to my mom, she replies with typical adult spin.
Each person develops at her own pace, Thaddeus, and that's perfectly O.K.
Mom, you and Dad gotta face facts. That baby's *dumb in the head.*
Thaddeus K. Fong: Martyr for Truth.

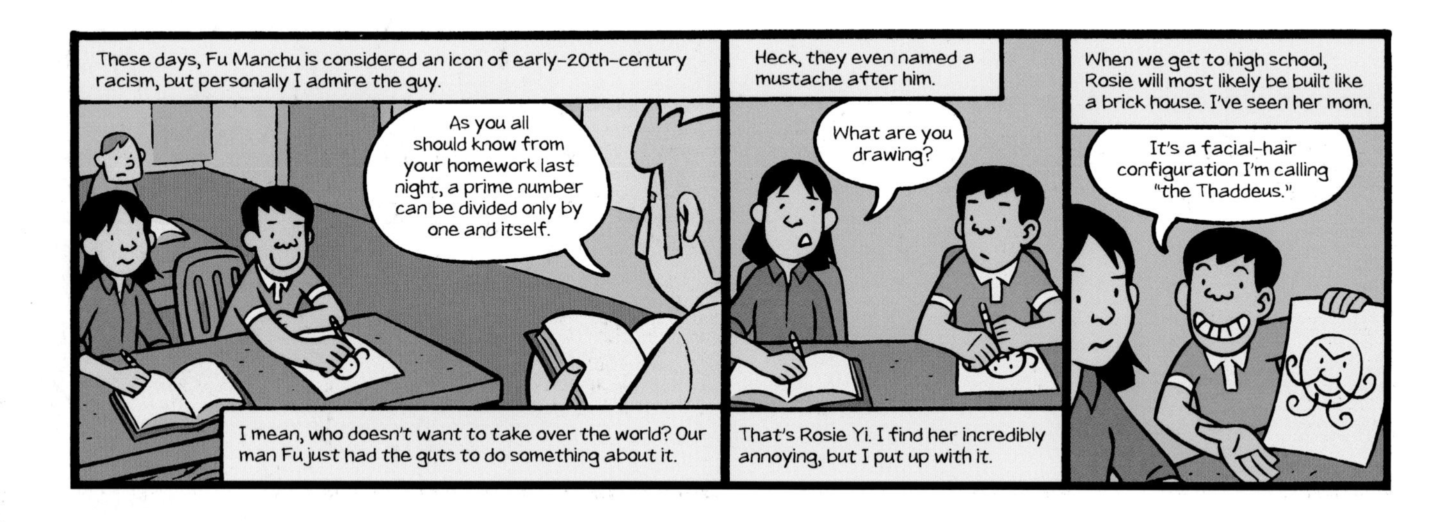
These days, Fu Manchu is considered an icon of early-20th-century racism, but personally I admire the guy.
As you all should know from your homework last night, a prime number can be divided only by one and itself.
I mean, who doesn't want to take over the world? Our man Fu just had the guts to do something about it.
Heck, they even named a mustache after him.
What are you drawing?
That's Rosie Yi. I find her incredibly annoying, but I put up with it.
When we get to high school, Rosie will most likely be built like a brick house. I've seen her mom.
It's a facial-hair configuration I'm calling "the Thaddeus."

I'm gonna grow one as soon as I hit puberty. Then once I become president of Planet Earth, I'm gonna make every male over the age of 13 grow one.
I'm planning to have a torrid affair with her 20 years from now, when my marriage to Miley Cyrus is on the rocks.
You're stupid.
Whatever.
After Rosie gets emotionally attached, I'll dump her like yesterday's laundry.
Thaddeus? Can you tell us what comes next?
Mr. Miller, you ridiculous little man. As if anything you say has any value to me whatsoever.
No, sir. I have no idea.

Seven, Thaddeus. Next is seven. Then 11, then 13. And there you have the first six prime numbers.
How's this ever gonna be useful in real life?
Ha, ha. Good one, Rosie. Maybe we can have a love child together before I break your heart.
I'm glad you asked, Ms. Yi. Prime numbers rarely occur in nature, but any society with reasonably developed mathematics can deduce what they are.
2 3 5 7
11 13
In fact, NASA scientists have theorized that if aliens were ever to make contact with us, it would be through prime numbers.
!
Mr. Miller! I stand corrected! You **have** taught me something of value!
You've taught me the truth about my baby sister.
1 Ga 2 ga
3 ga 4 ga 5 ga
6 ga 7 ga.

I devote my Saturday to carefully observing Maddie.
click.
Ga ga.
Two.
Ga ga ga.
Three.
Ga ga ga ga ga.
Five.

Ga ga ga ga ga ga ga.
Seven.
Ga ga ga ga ga ga ga ga ga ga ga.
Eleven.
Ga ga ga ga ga ga ga ga ga ga ga ga ga.
Thirteen.
It's so nice to see you two getting along, Thaddeus!
What-ever.

Ga ga ga ga ga ga ga ga ga ga ga ga ga ga ga ga ga.
Seventeen.
By early evening, I have enough data to confirm my suspicions.
They're all prime numbers!
click.
8:12 → 2
9:26 → 3
10:55 → 5
30 → 7
2:22 → 11
→ 13
My sister is an alien.

So what exactly are we looking at here, Sport?
This is a chart of Maddie's **ga**'s. Notice that they always come in a series, and the number of **ga**'s in a series is always a prime number! Don't you see the implications?!
"Prime number"?
* *Ugh!* *
A number that can be divided only by one and itself! Stay with me, Dad.
slap!
I don't remember learning stuff like that in third grade.
Dad, I'm smarter than you. I'm in accelerated math.
Watch your tone, Thaddeus! And can you please just get to the point? I have pilates in 20 minutes.

Fine. I'll spell it out for you: Your daughter is an alien.
What?!
I know this is a lot for you, Mom, since you had her living inside of you for nine months, but the same thing happened to Sigourney Weaver.
Ga ga ga ga ga ga ga ga ga ga ga ga ga ga ga ga ga ga ga.
See? Nineteen!
You've gotta call the F.B.I. and have them take her in for observation or dissection or something. I mean, who knows why she's on Earth? My own personal theory is that she's the harbinger of an invasion of—
Thaddeus!

Stop! I really thought you'd worked all this out already, what with the "big brother" present we gave you and all those sessions with Dr. Darby! I'm disappointed. We'll make another appointment with Dr. Darby tomorrow.
ARGH! Will you imbeciles get that baby drool out of your ears and listen to me?! We're talking about planetary security here!
!
Sometimes I find it hard to believe I actually emerged from that shallow, murky gene pool.
But it doesn't matter. They'll be sorry.
They'll be sorry when I'm elected president of Planet Earth. They'll be sorry when Maddie finally emerges from her humanoid shell and eats them. They'll be sorry they ever made me sit in the Naughty Chair.
And besides, I don't need them to heed my warning. Not when I have YouTube.

My parents bought this camcorder a couple of months before Maddie was born, intent on capturing every gas-induced smile she managed to eke out. They forbade me from ever touching it.
All right, Maddie. Do your thing.
As if what happened to the plasma screen was entirely my fault.
Ga ga ga.
Good. Keep going.
So I'm kind of disobeying my parents. So what? Excuse me for choosing the very survival of our species over their silly, small-minded rules.
Come on.
History will vindicate me.
Maddie! Pay attention! You know what comes next!
"Ga ga ga ga ga!"
!

Ga ga ga ga ga ga ga!
Good, good!
Now, "Ga ga ga ga ga ga ga ga ga ga ga!"
Ga ga ga ga ga ga ga ga ga ga ga ga ga!
Ew! What are you doing?!
Stop it! You're getting all your alien slime all over me!

Ga ga ga ga ga ga ga ga ga ga ga ga ga ga ga ga ga!
That's enough, Maddie. That'll do just fine.
Soon the world will know.
Heh, heh.
YouTub
Broadcast Yours
Video Uplo
Ga ga ga ga ga ga ga ga ga ga ga ga ga ga ga ga ga ga ga ga ga ga ga ga ga!
All right! Enough already!

YouTube
Broadcast Yourself
Worldwide
The Most Important Video Clip Ev
The Most Important Video Clip Ever!!!! by Thaddeus K. Fong!!!!
Congratulations, viewer! You are now watching the single-most-important video clip ever produced in the history of humankind!
At first glance, it will appear to be footage of an average human baby girl. But pay attention and count her ga's! Something nefarious is afoot!
Ga ga ga.

Ga ga ga ga ga ga ga!
Ga ga ga ga ga ga ga ga ga ga ga ga ga!
See? First 3, then 7, then 13! All prime numbers! How could a human baby possibly understand a complex mathematical concept like prime numbers, you ask?
The answer is ... your very question is flawed! She is *not* a human baby! She is in fact an alien, the harbinger of an extraterrestrial invasion of epic proportions!

Prepare yourselves, humanity! Prepare yourselves for *war!* This is Thaddeus K. Fong, signing off!
The Most Important Video Clip Ev
YouTube
Broadcast Yourself
Worldwide
The Most Important Video Clip Ev
A Thaddeus K. Fong Production!!!!
Oh, yeah, one more thing for the haters: I know it's hard to believe, but I did not edit that footage in any way. I swear.
The Most Important Video Clip Ev
The men in black should be arriving any minute now.

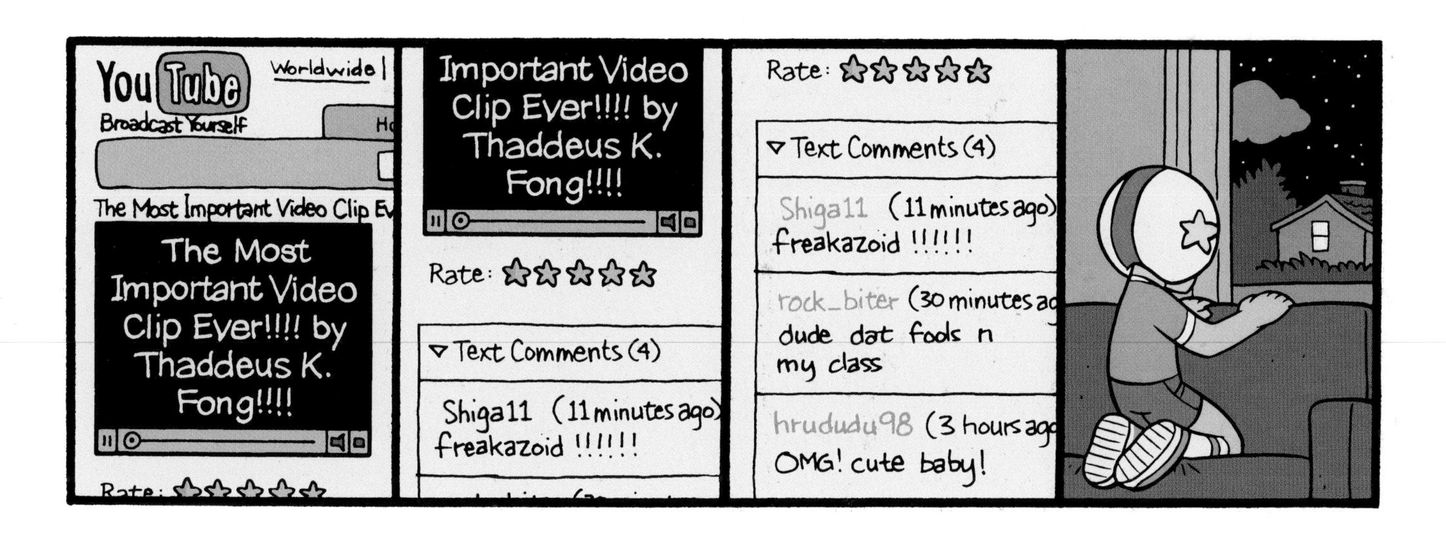

YouTube
Broadcast Yourself
Worldwide
The Most Important Video Clip Ev
The Most Important Video Clip Ever!!!! by Thaddeus K. Fong!!!!
Important Video Clip Ever!!!! by Thaddeus K. Fong!!!!
Rate:
Text Comments (4)
Shiga11 (11 minutes ago)
freakazoid !!!!!!
Rate:
Text Comments (4)
Shiga11 (11 minutes ago)
freakazoid !!!!!!
rock_biter (30 minutes ag
dude dat fools n my class
hrududu98 (3 hours ag
OMG! cute baby!

After uploading the video clip of the millennium to YouTube, I stayed up until 2 in the morning waiting for the F.B.I. to show up.
I'm still waiting.
Typical government bureaucrats. Probably caught up in paperwork.
I saw y-your video cl-cl-cl- **film** on the Internet last night.
Yeah?
Ever since Stuttering Stan beat me in the schoolwide spelling bee last year, he's been acting like he's my peer or something.
So s-s-seriously? Y-y-you think your sister's an al-al-al- **from outer space?**
The evidence speaks for itself.
His victory was a sheer accident. He won on "acquittance," and we both know it was his stutter, not his spelling prowess, that made him say the two t's.

Ha! You h-h-hear that?
Thaddeus, you're a nutjob!
It disgusts me to think that I lost the bee to a behavioral flaw. I try not to dwell on it.
A total nu-nu-nu- ***weirdo.***
Whatever.
You're even stupider than I thought.
Et tu, Rosie?

When it all goes down, these simpletons won't know what hit them.
We need one more to even out the teams for dodgeball.
How about Thaddeus?
I'll know it was an alien death ray.
Nah. Let's ask one of the second graders.
Dodgeball is kind of fun, though.

Later, nut job!
Ha h- h- ha!
Oh, look.
My parents have spent more of my inheritance on plastic toys for their alien baby. How nice.
Mmm!

Mm goo goo bwah!
What happened to "ga ga"?
Ya ya-
BLARF!
Finally, conclusive proof!
!!!
Mm ya bah!
THUMP
This is the best day of my life.
Dad? Where's Mom?
She's upstairs having her "Oprah" time. Let's leave her alone for a bit, O.K.?

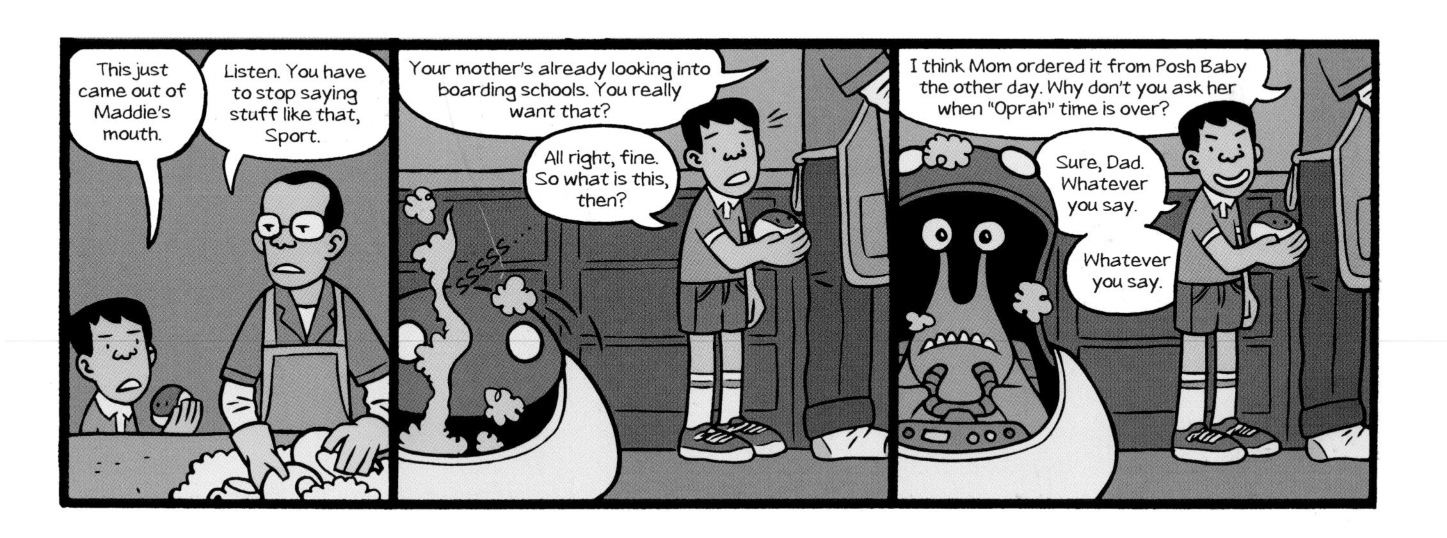
This just came out of Maddie's mouth.
Listen. You have to stop saying stuff like that, Sport.
Your mother's already looking into boarding schools. You really want that?
All right, fine. So what is this, then?
SSSSS...
I think Mom ordered it from Posh Baby the other day. Why don't you ask her when "Oprah" time is over?
Sure, Dad. Whatever you say.
Whatever you say.

It has been several hours since the alien slugs emerged from their space pods, and all they've done is watch the television in the Yoga room.
. . . and now here's your host, Conan O'Brien!
They're gathering intelligence about the world they plan to conquer, no doubt.
All the better for me. It gives me more time to prepare for our apocalyptic confrontation.
I'll lure them out to the public square by City Hall, where there's plenty of space for reporters and camera crews.
Bring it on!

There, I will battle them for days, destroying all the surrounding government buildings in the process.
POW!
Finally, at high noon on a hot, windless Sunday, I'll vanquish the last of the invaders with my Thadde-o-Ray.™
Eat highly focused light, slime bucket!
ZAP!
Of all my arsenal, the Thadde-o-Ray™ was the most difficult to construct.
High-powered flashlight
Magnifying glasses, glued together
Water-gun handle
But clearly, it'll be worth it.

My parents—and all the world—will adore me forever.
What a guy!
He's the best thing I ever gave birth to!
My presidency of Planet Earth will be all but assured.
Miley, *please!* Not in front of the cameras!
Bap mmm?
Ya ya bap mmm ya!
After all those space pods came out of her, Maddie has inexplicably become a normal baby.
Which is totally fine by me. She's no longer part of the equation.
Maddie, leave me alone!

It's just past midnight when I finally finish both my costume and arsenal.
I've decided this is the perfect opportunity to introduce the world to "the Thaddeus," that mustache I invented.
I needed a little help from my mom's eyeliner. Notoriety does not wait for puberty, unfortunately.

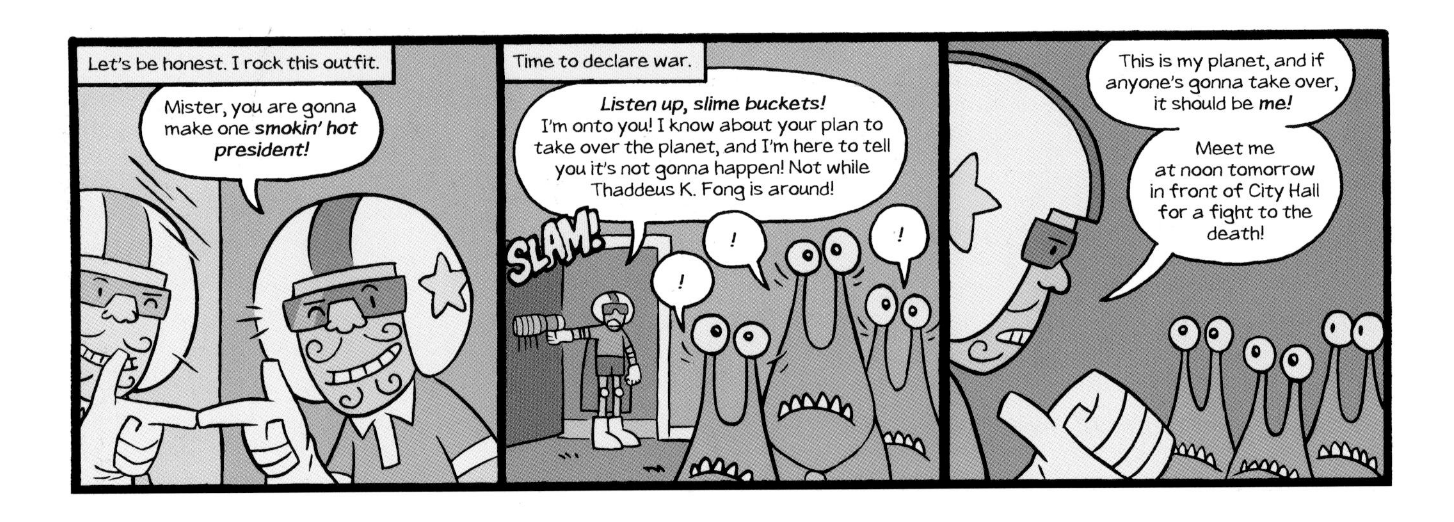
Let's be honest. I rock this outfit.
Mister, you are gonna make one smokin' hot president!
Time to declare war.
Listen up, slime buckets! I'm onto you! I know about your plan to take over the planet, and I'm here to tell you it's not gonna happen! Not while Thaddeus K. Fong is around!
SLAM!
!
!
!
This is my planet, and if anyone's gonna take over, it should be me!
Meet me at noon tomorrow in front of City Hall for a fight to the death!

Friend... you do not... understand... We are... mission... mission...
You're on a mission to take control of Earth, I know!
No, we are... **missionaries!** Missionaries of ☺☺☼♡!
Roughly translated: Missionaries of smiles and happy feelings!
We do not... fight... We bring... smiles and happy feelings!

ZAP!
NO! Brother!
WHUMP!
Slap.
We forgive you.
This is not how things are supposed to go.

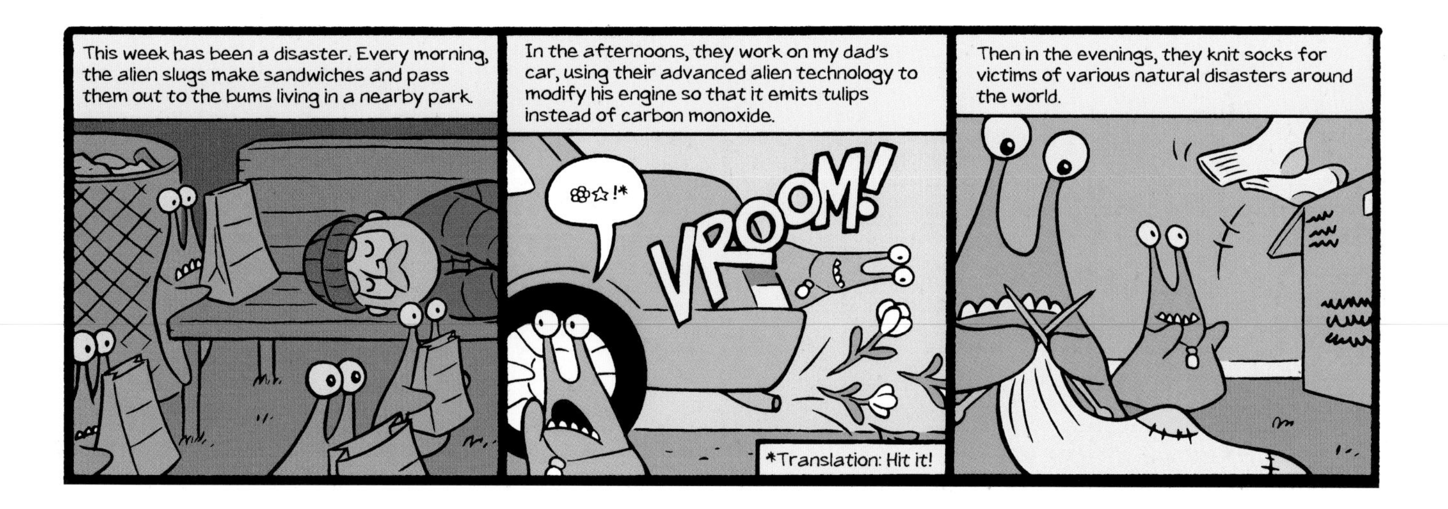
This week has been a disaster. Every morning, the alien slugs make sandwiches and pass them out to the bums living in a nearby park.
In the afternoons, they work on my dad's car, using their advanced alien technology to modify his engine so that it emits tulips instead of carbon monoxide.
VROOM!
*Translation: Hit it!
Then in the evenings, they knit socks for victims of various natural disasters around the world.

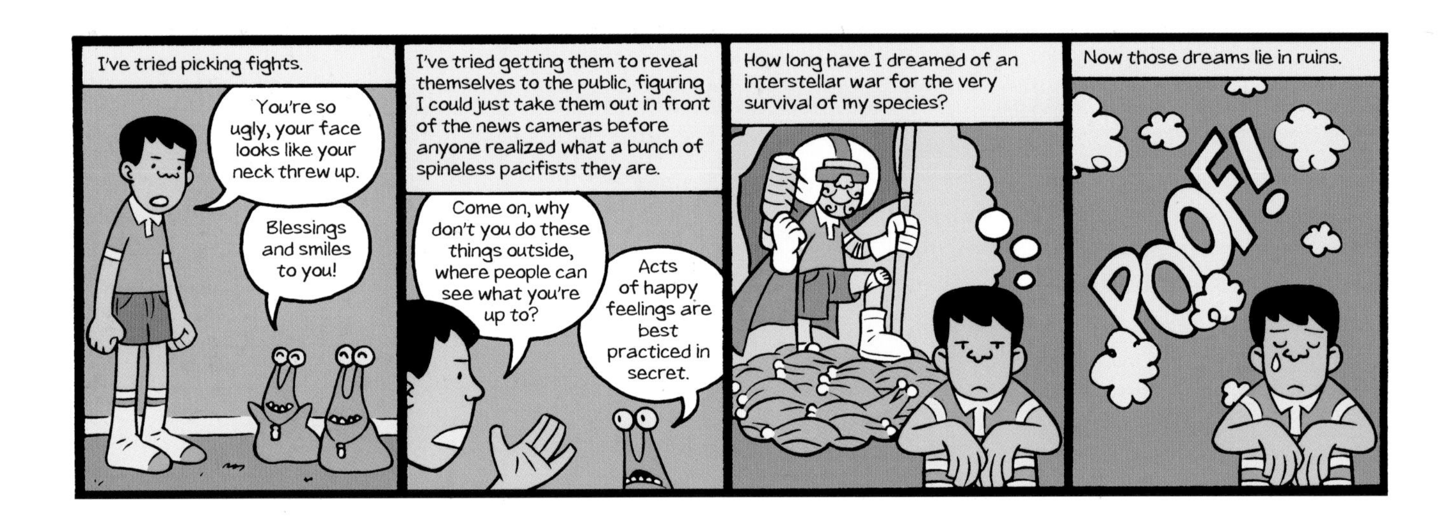
I've tried picking fights.
You're so ugly, your face looks like your neck threw up.
Blessings and smiles to you!
I've tried getting them to reveal themselves to the public, figuring I could just take them out in front of the news cameras before anyone realized what a bunch of spineless pacifists they are.
Come on, why don't you do these things outside, where people can see what you're up to?
Acts of happy feelings are best practiced in secret.
How long have I dreamed of an interstellar war for the very survival of my species?
Now those dreams lie in ruins.
POOF!

Thaddeus, why so sad? Perhaps you'd like to join us for our nightly singalong?
Go die.
You know where to find us if you change your mind.
Blessings and smiles to you!
I've got peace like a river, I've got peace like a river, I've got peace like a river in my pneumostome!
Goo ba mmm ya ya!
rattle rattle

Alien slugs have infested my house for weeks now, and my parents are as oblivious as ever.
Mom, look.
Honey, quick! Get the camcorder!
They're blinded by baby fat.
Maddie has the hiccups!
Ha ha! So cute!
hic!
Hey. How exactly did you guys end up coming out of my sister's mouth? Is she like an alien slug factory or something?
She is a gateway between dimensions.

"Gateways are born randomly into species on different planets, in different dimensions. The Missionaries of Smiles and Happy Feelings monitor these gateways very carefully.
Ga ga ga ga ga.
"More often than not, the species they are born into are not ready for our message. They haven't yet evolved the capacity for *souls* or the facial muscles for *smiles*.
Ga ga ga ga ga.
?
"But every now and then, we receive a response. Then it is time to get to work!"
Ga ga ga ga ga ga ga.
!
!*
*Translation: Ready the space pods!

Soon, smiles and happy feelings will fill the corners of the multiverse!
Yay!
So there are more of you where you came from?
Yes. Many more.
Will more of you be coming here?
If there is need.
My plans for the presidency of Planet Earth may have been delayed by a decade or so, but at least I can still do something about Maddie.

...peace like a—
Thaddeus! What happened to your socks?
Someone stole them from me at school. It was horrible!
No! Why?!
Haven't you heard? There's a planetary sock shortage! Soon there'll be riots in the streets over socks!
But Conan O'Brien made no mention of any such thing!

Look at my feet! My cold, bare feet! Would I lie to you about something like this?!
If only an army of kindhearted souls would come to our planet and knit enough socks for everyone!
☺☆✿ ☼◎✿✿✿ ◎◎☼♡♡☺ ☺☺☺☺!*
Goo ya!
*Translation: Brothers, it's time to call in the cavalry!
Maddie, you have no idea what you're in for.
Mmm ya ya!

Hey, Mom? I think something's wrong with Maddie.
Thaddeus! If you-
Look!
BLARF!
BLARF!
BLARF!
BLARF!
. . .

My parents took Maddie to the emergency room last week. During the examination, the doctor accidentally dropped her tongue depressor into the alien slug dimension. Government agents were called in.
Maddie's now being kept in a secret underground research facility, accessible only through a fake wall in the broom closet of a Vietnamese nail salon downtown.
The space pods have been sent three floors below, where a group of eggheads are undoubtedly wetting their pants over them.
Excuse me, ma'am.
Again, Jones?
So sorry, ma'am. It's just too exciting.
My parents insist on visiting her every day. Even with the 12-inch-thick Plexiglas wall separating us from Maddie, they make us wear Hazmat suits.
Hazmat suits! ***So awesome.***

Back home, I indulge in my favorite pastime ever: planning my next birthday. So what if it's 10 months away?
Hey, Dad, can I get a a new bike for my birthday?
Sure, Sport.
How about a Sherman tank?
Sure, Sport.
A small island republic I can rule with an iron fist?
Sure, Sport.
I have to say, my parents' emotional distress is not without its benefits.

Can I borrow your credit card?
Whatever you want, Sport.
ebaY®
Categories
Motors
Stores
SMALL ISLAND REPUB
Buy It Now: $360,000,

Th-Th-Thaddeus?
What do you want?
I saw th-that thing about the b-b-b- *infant* last night on the n-news.
...the American people have a right to know! It's just too exciting! The baby's parents claim she spat the pod up, but we're pretty sure it's extraterrestrial in origin!
Um, you're positive my face won't show, right?
Really. The public knows, then.
So they were talking about your sister?
Yes.
My prospects for imminent world domination have unexpectedly revived.

Your sister's *actually* an al- al- al- **from outer space?**
Technically, no. She's more of a gateway to another dimension, a portal aliens use to go from their world to ours.
Then... there really *is* going to be an invasion?
Ha! The invasion's already begun, people! *The invasion's already begun!*
An invasion of smiles and happy feelings, but they don't need to know that.
More likely than not, only half of us will still be alive in a year.
* Sh-sh-shudder *
What do we do, Thaddeus?! I want to live!
I'll tell you *exactly* what to do... right after a game of *dodge-ball!* I'm on Rosie's team!
I guess...
She loves me.

OOF!
Ha, ha! Tell me, Stan, how many P's are there in "whupped"?
WHAM!
Suddenly, without really meaning to or wanting to, I recognize that look Maddie gave me during our last visit to the research facility.
Loneliness.
WHAM!

What the-?!
You lied to us!
We called in countless missionaries to spend countless hours knitting countless socks, all to relieve a worldwide sock shortage that doesn't even exist! We are so *angry!*
But we forgive you.
Yeah.

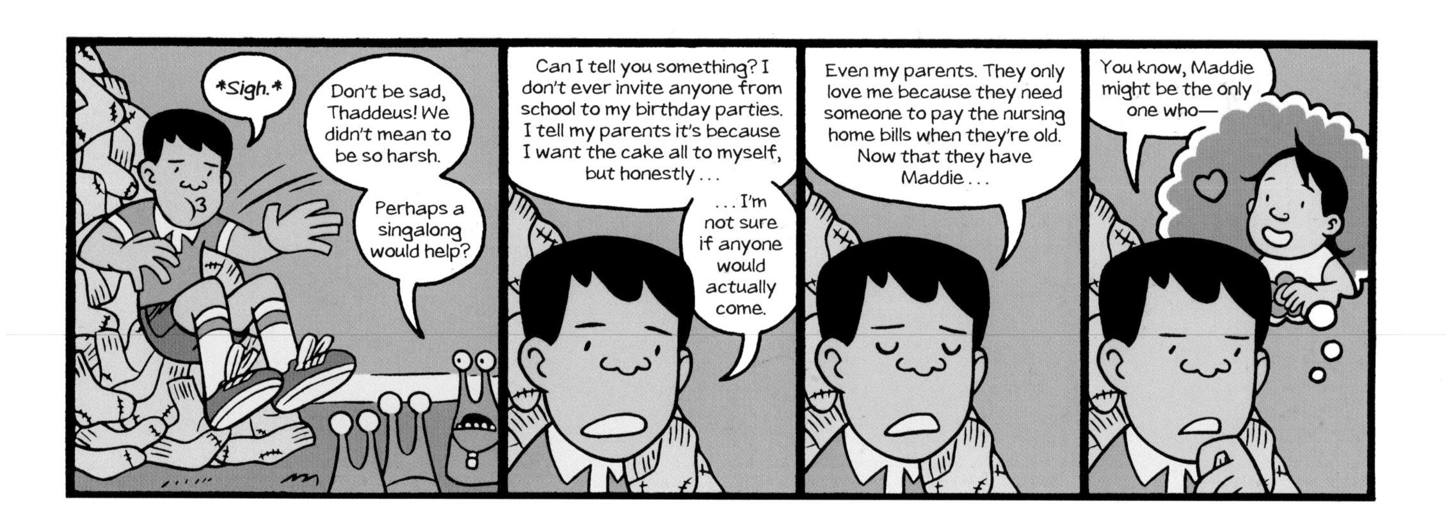
Sigh.
Don't be sad, Thaddeus! We didn't mean to be so harsh.
Perhaps a singalong would help?
Can I tell you something? I don't ever invite anyone from school to my birthday parties. I tell my parents it's because I want the cake all to myself, but honestly . . .
. . . I'm not sure if anyone would actually come.
Even my parents. They only love me because they need someone to pay the nursing home bills when they're old. Now that they have Maddie . . .
You know, Maddie might be the only one who—

Ew, gross! What are you doing?!
You're gonna get your outerspace germs on me!
We're being with you, Thaddeus. We're being in your presence.
Sometimes, the best way to bring about smiles and happy feelings in a person is to simply be with him—
—and feel what he feels.
Nobody likes me. I'm so sad.

After Maddie was taken to the secret underground research facility, my parents swept through our house gathering up all the space pods they could find.
They handed them over to the government, hoping it might get Maddie released sooner.
Yeah. As if the government ever does anything "sooner."

Ha!
I knew it!
Just as I'd hoped. My parents missed one.
But did it have to be behind the toilet?
. . . to
feel what she
feels.

Hey, Mom.
Look.
Not now, Thaddeus. I've got a lot on my–
PTUI.
...

At the secret underground research facility, they put me in the same room as Maddie because we have the same freaky "condition."
Goo ba ya!
It took her a bit to warm up to me again. But just a bit.
Maddie, that's enough. It's time to be serious.
I introduced her to the Thaddeus a few days ago. She immediately took to it.
Hold still.
I have to redraw it every day because of her drool.

I hate to admit it, but despite being a baby and a female, Maddie rocks the Thaddeus.
Ha, ha!
Mmm ma!
It has made me reconsider my political positions. Perhaps it's sexist of me to require only males to grow the Thaddeus after I become president of Planet Earth.
My parents still visit us every day, looking as worried as ever.
I'm sure that'll stop once that small island republic shows up on their credit-card bill.

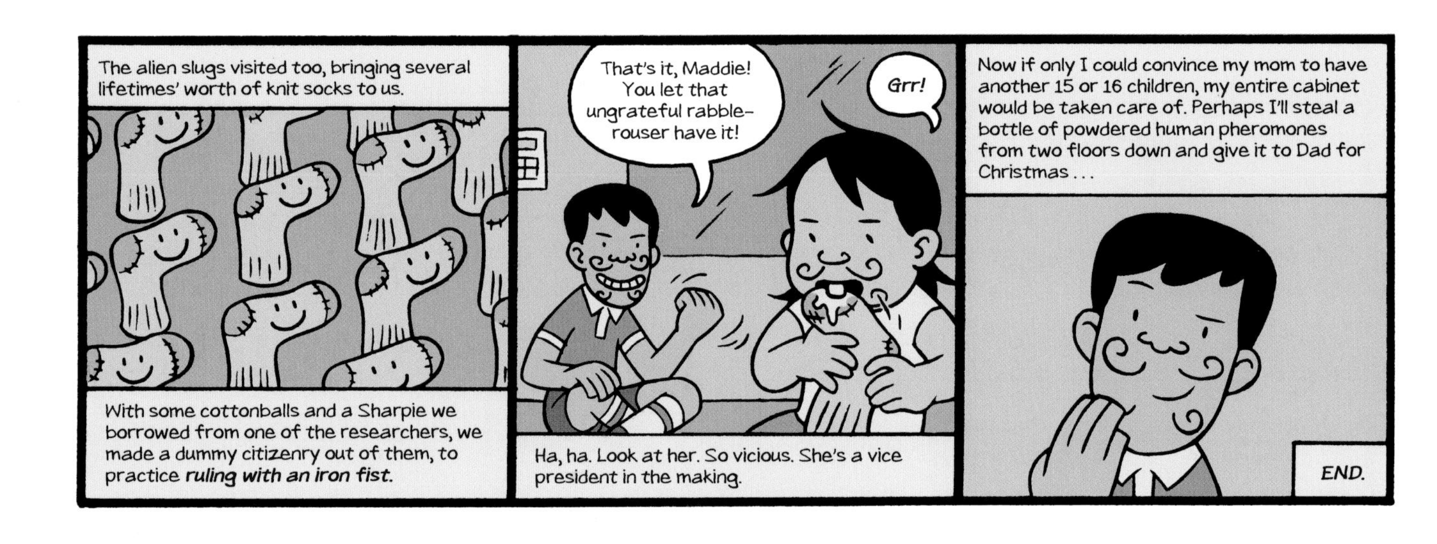
The alien slugs visited too, bringing several lifetimes' worth of knit socks to us.
With some cottonballs and a Sharpie we borrowed from one of the researchers, we made a dummy citizenry out of them, to practice ***ruling with an iron fist.***
That's it, Maddie! You let that ungrateful rabble-rouser have it!
Grr!
Ha, ha. Look at her. So vicious. She's a vice president in the making.
Now if only I could convince my mom to have another 15 or 16 children, my entire cabinet would be taken care of. Perhaps I'll steal a bottle of powdered human pheromones from two floors down and give it to Dad for Christmas . . .
END.

First Second
New York & London

Published by First Second,
First Second is an imprint of Roaring Brook Press, a division of Holtzbrinck Publishing Holdings Limited Partnership,
175 Fifth Avenue, New York, NY 10010

Distributed in Canada by H. B. Fenn and Company Ltd.
distributed in the United Kingdom by Macmillan Children's Books, a division of Pan Macmillan.

Colored by Derek Kirk Kim
Design by Colleen AF Venable

Cataloging-in-Publication Data is on file at the Library of Congress.
ISBN: 978-1-59643-612-1
COLLECTOR'S EDITION ISBN: 978-1-59643-650-3

First Second books are available for special promotions and premiums. For details, contact: Director of Special Markets, Holtzbrinck Publishers.

First Edition April 2010
Printed in China
10 9 8 7 6 5 4 3 2 1